TREASURE

of

TRUTHS

REBECCA
HAINES

Drop
Cap
Publishing

Copyright © 2012 Drop Cap Publishing
Design: David Hoover
Editor, publicity: Cody Dyer

For information, address:
Drop Cap Publishing
2139 S. Maple
Carthage, MO 64836
www.dropcappublishing.com

ISBN-13: 978-0615726694
ISBN-10: 0615726690

PRINTED IN THE UNITED STATES OF AMERICA

This book is dedicated to
Grandmother Lottie Mathews.
Thank you for believing in all of us.

PRELUDE

"Taste the bitter sweetness of victory!" yelled Captain Rifton to his crew as the ocean's furious blows hit the ship side-by-side their enemies' cannons.

"Tonight we will reap what was so rightfully ours seven years ago!" the captain shouted as he grabbed hold of a rope. Gracefully swinging onto the enemy's vessel, Captain Rifton held his sword to his enemy's chest, "We meet again old friend . . . but this time, you won't have the chance to do any backstabbing."

1

Two young lovers, John Rifton and Constance Brisco, set their hearts on running away to the wild, open sea. The starry-eyed dreamers had originated from wealthy families, but desired much more from life than what was already planned for them in the monotonous township of Dorchelle.

Times were exciting—small civilizations like Dorchelle were sprouting throughout the Caribbean. Streams of people by the masses migrated across the oceans which brought great riches, but also attracted pirates from the far reaches of the world.

The night before Constance was to betroth another suitor, she promised John, an up-and-coming young accountant, she would meet him at the docks.

Neither of them had planned on such an outrageous endeavor, but everything fell into place when the two met and shared their lives' aspirations far away from judgmental ears.

John had arranged for the Hestia, a swift schooner, to wait for them at the docks. This impressive vessel was captained by John's close friend, Darion Hoggard. The two had known each other for years, but had lived different lives until now. The friends were reunited at sea with the accompaniment of the lovely lady, Constance.

Darion had recruited some robust, fighting men for his crew. All were seasoned veterans of the sea, and wouldn't know how to live any other way. Of course being the hearty pirates they were, there were always fights, a bet gone wrong, or one too many words said in disgust.

Constance quickly adapted to the ways of the pirates, but was successful in keeping her distance. John was always there to protect her, and together they learned the trade of sailing. In their first months at sea, while the crew slaked their thirst for rum, John would enjoy conversations with the older, and more experienced pirates who told the greatest stories of their ventures. This was how he acquired ideas for navigating, reading the weather, and battle strategies; which he secretly found to be lacking in Darion's command.

Nevertheless, the Hestia was victorious in battles against other pirate ships and reaped the benefits of gold and silver whenever possible. When the situation arose for fighting, John and Constance were thrown into the crusades with no other choice but to survive. The young woman quickly found her casual dresses were anything but appropriate for such a life, but she kept a couple with the hope that she could still feel like a lady when not scrubbing the port bow.

Before Constance lived a pirate's life, she enjoyed looking beautiful with her long, dark hair fastened upward. Sometimes she would even have her handmaiden weave a vibrant ribbon through her curls. Her father, as the one of the most prestigious ambassadors of Dorchelle, found bright ribbons to be over exuberant. However, he found controlling his wild-hearted daughter a long lost cause.

Constance wistfully caressed the expensive materials of one of her favorite dresses, which were stored in an old, wooden chest in the hull of the Hestia. She could still hear the graceful tunes of a quartet playing a lively song for her and her fiancé. He was a handsome man, and a smug individual who prioritized marriage after a successful career. Constance's father liked him and his "down to earth views," as he called them. Constance smiled at the memory of singeing the lace of her wedding gown with the end of a cigarette.

Shaking Constance from her memories, John called to her from the quarterdeck.

"There's a treasure, Constance," John said with shining brown eyes. "A treasure so great we could live like royalty for the rest of our lives, and just sail forever into a never-ending sunset."

Completely interested and entertained by her love's poetry, Constance smiled and urged him to continue.

"Earning it will be the trick, but we can do it . . . it's on the Isle de Flamo in the southern waters. Half the island has been searched for years for this treasure, and every treasure seeker has given up, or gone as far as they could . . . because the other half of the island is a volcano."

Constance's green eyes widened, "A volcano. You want to search a volcano?"

"It's not in the volcano, it's on the other side . . ." John started to explain.

"But no one can get to the other side because it's

impossible to maneuver through the dangerous reef," interrupted Darion, sitting down next to the two. "We'll have to go when the volcano isn't erupting . . . which isn't long."

"It's not as active as it once was," John insisted. "I've heard the island is growing cooler by the year. And it won't be too much longer before we can get to the other side, and find a treasure beyond our imaginations."

Constance's shoulders sank, "But the longer we wait, the longer someone else will have to try to get it first."

"You're starting to think like a pirate!" Darion laughed.

"But I don't understand," Constance laughed, "how could a great treasure like this get left behind?"

"Legend has it," John started, "Captain Darkhaven gathered all this treasure and was going to share it with the one he loved . . . He killed every member of his crew by burning them alive in the volcano."

Shivering a bit, Constance grimaced, "How romantic . . ."

"Well," Darion said, "I heard he died on that cursed island waiting for a girl that was never gonna show up anyway."

"Oh how awful," Constance gasped.

"Whether she died on her way to him, or had never intended to meet him on the Isle de Flamo, either way, the treasure is still there," John said, reassuring the goal of their future voyage.

The three shared a moment of high spirits, but were soon feeling a strong sense of determination. Just hearing of such a challenge made Constance want it; wanting to share it with the one he loved made John want it; and hearing a person of John's caliber speak of the legend made Darion want it. The treasure of the Isle de Flamo may have been a myth, but it was the most sought after fortune of its time. Just thinking of it gave Darion a thrill and he briskly left the two lovers.

"That treasure is going to be how we'll be able to spend our lives together at sea in peace," holding Constance's dainty hands in his, John said, "I promise to find the Isle de Flamo, and enjoy the fortune with you for the rest of our lives."

2

In the galley of the Hestia one humid, sunny day, Constance peeled potato after potato. At the other side of the muggy room, a corpulent pirate by the name of MeLoy stirred a thick substance in a large pot.

"It is stifling in here," Constance exhaled. "Do you ever intend to speak with me?"

The man kept his back turned to the young lady, keeping his even rhythm in stirring. Constance wondered for a moment if he had even heard her. She pushed up her sleeves and wiped her brow with the upper part of her hand, just gazing across the galley at MeLoy's back. She continued to peel another potato, and glanced back at her slowly diminishing pile.

"We've lived on this ship for months now . . . almost a year," Constance said, hoping for a response sooner or later. "You've spoken to John, but not to me . . . Do I make you nervous?"

When she still received no response, she simply smiled and looked back at her peeling.

"You know, John told me of a belief that some of the

men have," Constance inquired. "They say, having a woman aboard could annoy the evil spirits of the sea."

Constance noticed MeLoy's hand quiver slightly in his stirring, but he still said nothing.

"Are you a superstitious man, MeLoy?" Constance mocked in a playful tone. "It was always my thought having a useless woman aboard would anger the spirits . . ."

This statement caused a pause in MeLoy's stirring.

"Wouldn't it make sense that bringing something worthless onboard would go against the spirits of the waters?" Constance questioned aloud. "Now, bringing aboard something that works, thinks, and fights for the glory of the ship . . . if anything, that should please them . . . Don't you think?"

Constance watched the man's shoulders shrug, and then he turned around. She was in the middle of a peel when he raised a brow at her.

"Ya know, you make a lot of sense thar lassie," MeLoy said in a deep tone, then gave the girl an accepting wink.

It was only moments after the two finally conversed that they heard the captain's shouts of alarm. MeLoy removed the huge pot from its heat and Constance pounded her knife into the table upright; in a flash they were on the main deck.

"Get to yar battle stations!" ordered Darion from behind the helm. "Ready the long cannons!"

Constance burst across the deck as the ship sprang to life with activity. She collided with another pirate, and looked up to see it was John.

"I'll fetch gun powder!" she shouted.

"Stay down and keep out of the way!" John ordered in a stressful tone.

They quickly parted, and John dashed up to the

quarterdeck. Squinting his eyes from the sun, he took one more look at the fast oncoming opponent.

"Darion! We should be putting to full sail! Our cannons won't reach them from here, but our speed could catch them off-guard!" John pleaded in fury.

"Thank you for your suggestions Mr. Rifton, now prepare the long cannons!" boomed Darion's angry demand.

John turned back to see the engaging ship turn to fire as Darion began to turn the Hestia hard to return the attack. The first cannonball made a splash in front of the ship, but the next was a direct hit near the figurehead of the Hestia. Darion gave the order to fire, but as John predicted, the cannons' shots fell short of the enemy. Directly after the near misses, the Hestia suffered another blow.

"She's big and slow!" laughed Darion as he turned the ship toward the vessel.

John bolted to help the men reloading the long cannons. In a swift motion he then helped prepare the midrange cannons for the closer battle about to happen in moments.

The two ships passed each other through swift waters, each doing tremendous damage to the other. The mystery ship still had the upper hand as it turned and rapidly discharged enormous firepower on the Hestia.

Constance was knocked to the deck as pieces of the ship were blown to splinters. She looked up to see John firing a pistol, along with every other crew member firing close range weapons. The loudness of the battle made Constance's eardrums feel as though they were on fire inside her head. She cupped them with her hands and stayed down.

After an hour of battle, crew members of the Hestia were aboard the other vessel fighting the last of the enemy. Constance opened her eyes and slowly stood up as pirates dodged her on the deck. She gasped at the sight of the devastated ship. In such a short amount of time, the immaculate vessel was now a floating heap of rubble.

"Cap'n!" called a scurvy, one-eyed man from the enemy's burning ship.

Constance looked to her side and saw Darion and John gazing back at the caller.

"What do ye want wit de surviviors?!" the man asked in a raspy voice across the water.

With little hesitation, Darion called back, "Thar are no survivors."

Not saying a word, John looked at his old friend in frustrated confusion.

"Johnny boy," whispered Darion, "question my orders?"

John still said nothing as Constance watched this conversation intently.

"Go salvage what you can from that ship, take no prisoners, and come back to help repair the ship," Darion said in a monotone. "This is a victory . . . and we'll soon make port to celebrate . . . Tell the men."

With that, Darion left the main deck and disappeared down the stairs. John could feel his face turn red and his teeth grit, but he grabbed hold of a rope and swung onto the slowly sinking ship. Constance could hear the ship breaking, the crew scavenging every inch and cheerfully finding items of use. Then, she heard the echoing sounds of pistol shots, signaling the discovery of survivors and their executions. She thought to herself, "This is what it's all about, but it doesn't feel right."

3

For days Darion and John did not exchange a single word. The crew's morale hung on the anticipation of the nearing day when their port full of shady characters, gambling, liquor, and vulgar women would appear on the horizon. Constance spoke to a select few of the crew members; with the help of MeLoy, she had persuaded some of the men her presence on the ship was not going to upset any evil spirits.

Lately, John was a man of few words with everyone, even when Constance tried to talk of the treasure. His silence gave Constance the impression he was in denial the sea had turned his friend into a heartless buccaneer; however, it was only a guess.

The evening grew long, and Constance finished her work in the galley. She reached the top of the stairs to the main deck, and felt a smile stretch across her face at the beauty of the sunset. She took a deep breath, glancing around and noticed a lone figure peering off the railing. Looking to the east, Darion stood alone. As though he were a wounded, dangerous animal, Constance approached him.

"Evening," she greeted quietly.

"Yes it is," was his deep reply, not looking at her.

"I've noticed you and John aren't speaking," Constance started.

"So he sent you to make peace," Darion half smiled, with tension in his voice.

"That's not it at all," Constance said sternly. "I was simply making conversation . . . I didn't realize you two were at war."

"Men are always at war, Constance," Darion sneered, glaring at her. "I don't expect you to understand that. But what I don't see, is how we'll ever retrieve a treasure on that cursed island."

"Is that all that is bothersome to you?" Constance asked, bewildered and angered. "Your best friend isn't speaking to you, and all you can think of is the treasure?!"

As she was turning to leave, Darion caught her arm and pulled her close violently.

"Tell your man to come speak to me and we'll put this all behind us . . . He questioned my orders, and though you may think of us as a ruthless bunch, we have rules aboard this ship . . . and no one questions the captain."

Constance moved her arm slightly to try to twist out of his grip, but looked back into his glaring eyes. She had always thought of Darion as an attractive man, but this threatening gesture gave him a new image in her mind.

"You are a beautiful woman, Constance," Darion whispered. "Out here at sea, we all just do what we have to do to survive . . . Are you a survivor?"

Not knowing how to answer, Constance yanked her

arm free from his grasp. They stared at each other for a moment then Constance quickly left.

That night, she decided not to tell John about the encounter other than to mention Darion wanted to speak with him. Before falling asleep, Constance told herself there was no point in explaining something that probably meant nothing.

On the dawning of the next day, a skinny pirate known as ScottyD swung down from the sails of the ship. He was known to the crew as a language extraordinaire, and a sharp-witted scoundrel at that.

"If me eyes serve me justly," ScottyD chatted to whoever would listen. "We should be coming in to port in four hours."

"Very good," Darion remarked, gazing up at the wind-filled sails. "This round I need a good boatswain . . . Get her looking respectable again."

"And who should be the so auspicious individual, sir?" ScottyD asked with a playful bow.

"Johnny boy," Darion answered, after he turned and saw his old friend observing the sails' ragged tears.

Putting an arm around John's shoulders, Darion led him away from the others.

"We're all after the same thing, Rifton," Darion said, "you, me, the crew . . . Constance. We all do what we must, right?"

John was silent, but nodded in agreement.

"After you prove yourself to the crew what kind of a man you are by whipping this creaking tub back into shape, you won't have to question my orders during a battle," Darion stated.

"It was not my intention to question your leadership, Darion," John said firmly.

"Good," Darion said, but kept his piercing blue eyes fixed on the open sea. "Now that we have that behind us, I've been wondering about the treasure . . ."

At first, John was concerned how fast the conversation had turned, but soon was reassured all was well by his friend's excited smile—the same smile he remembered from years ago.

"It's my guess the Isle de Flamo will be tame in about seven years," John explained. "From what I've heard, the island is relatively small, and it won't be easy for our larger men to move around in those caverns. Maybe we can recruit some shorter fellows—would prove more efficient."

"Brilliant," Darion complimented. "That's why you're a top dog at sea, Johnny boy!"

As Darion walked down the stairs, Constance was coming up. They didn't exchange glances as Constance's gaze met her love's happy eyes. John put his arm around her delicate waist.

"We'll be at the next port in no time," John said with a smile.

"Wonderful," Constance smiled with a sigh of relief. "Are we also repairing the ship?"

"Yes, and guess who was placed in charge of it?" John asked, as if she needed more than one guess.

"That is marvelous!" she said, feeling a huge weight lifted off her shoulders.

The day continued on like a well-oiled machine. The weather was picture perfect, and the port was able to supply everything the Hestia needed, and more. As John oversaw the ship's refurbishment, he noticed Darion recruited some new members. Though they were not small or short, John still considered them to be credible assets to the ship, and they proved their worth.

A few days on land was always a time of relaxation for Constance, but this time she was just glad to see Darion and John were on good terms again.

4

Plans to set sail the following morning meant it was the last night to live life to the fullest for the rowdy crew. The men grew louder and louder as the night carried on at the local tavern. It was well-known the Hestia was not a welcomed ship.

"Your men always trash my place and kill any good help I have when you come to port!" was the blunt, firm statement from the lady tavern owner known as Calina, from behind the bar to Darion. Once she was informed he was the captain, she showed no fear in expressing her disdain for the crew.

"They drive business away," she glared as she leaned across the bar.

"My men are thirsty and require some attention of the feminine persuasion," Darion sneered, as he took a drink from a metal stein with his gaze in every direction but at the tavern owner. "Who am I to deny them of that on their last night in your lovely corner of the sea?"

As Calina took a breath to rebuttal, Darion stepped away and she lost sight of him immediately in the crowd.

In a fit of rage, she crushed a small glass onto the bar under her callused hand—without a flinch—and stormed upstairs.

Constance sat with a straight back, clearly uncomfortable in the filthy scene. Darion had insisted John attend the night's festivities to improve his "camaraderie with the crew."

"Oh that's ridiculous," Constance retorted when John told her of Darion's persistence. "You get along just fine with the crew."

From across the smoky room, John and Constance's attention focused on two struggling figures close to the staircase. A brute of a man named Triggs was intoxicated and grabbed one of the bar maidens by the arm. She did her best not to spill the tray of drinks, but when Triggs shoved her the tray made a startling crash. Enraged, the maiden tried to push Triggs away. With a laugh, Triggs slapped the girl and she fell to the floor.

Despite Constance's late pleas, John was already up out of his chair and approaching Triggs.

"Why don't you find a drink at the bar my friend," John asked the man who stood a good foot taller than he.

"Why don't you mind your own business?" Triggs blurted, doing his best to pronounce each syllable.

Constance sunk in her chair as she watched the conversation go nowhere fast.

Triggs drew his sword on John, who found himself defenseless. He swayed out of harm's way with each of Triggs' stumbling thrusts. The crowd quickly formed a circle around the two, delighted to witness the duel. Many in the boisterous crowd cheered for Triggs; hearing his fans, his advances became more determined. John treated the match like a game with a child, but drew a hot poker from the fireplace to protect himself in case his opponent got lucky.

The two exchanged attacks, each blocking each other successfully as the poker and the sword made loud clangs with each strike. But, from somewhere in the indefinite crowd, came a freshly-sharpened knife at John's waist. At the last moment, John quickly turned to avoid the blade, and in doing so he slashed the scolding poker across Triggs' face.

The sound and smell of the roasting eye chilled John's spine and sent a quiver through the crowd. Grimacing at the sound of Triggs' scream of agonizing pain, the tavern fell silent and made a path for the man to flee.

Shocked and guilty, John threw the poker back into the fireplace. As everyone watched, John quietly walked out of the tavern as Constance took his arm by the door.

5

Weeks passed since the Hestia weighed anchor at the last port, and now struggled against the sea's ferocious winds and spraying tides. John was taking a shift as the helmsman when the storm approached, and had requested Darion's presence to prepare. But even unprepared, the ship was young and strong. He had no time to be angered by the reckless crew as he strongly positioned the helm with all his might.

"Steady boys! It only gets smoother from here!" John yelled to the men, who were scrambling to perform their duties to steady the ship.

In the hold of the rocking ship, crew members fought to secure supplies. In the captain's cabin, Constance attempted to secure maps and other papers. She, John and Darion had spoken of navigating through the southern waters just the previous night; but now, the important documents were in danger with the ship rocking so violently. Suddenly, the door swung open and Constance looked up to see it was Darion. Preoccupied with the papers, Constance kept her balance.

"What needs done?" she asked her friend. "As soon as these are secure, I'll be free to go up on deck, or wherever!"

Without saying a word, Darion stood in the spontaneous flashes of the storm's light show. With all the commotion of the merciless weather, Constance felt excited and almost lighthearted. But all those feelings were lost when she looked up to see Darion shut the door behind him. She felt a wave of different emotions shiver down her spine—making her feel threatened, confused and afraid. He took the maps from the silent, young woman's hands and tossed them aside. The ship suddenly shifted as Constance tried to bolt for the door, and they both fell to the floor. In the scramble, Constance whipped her elbow around in Darion's face, but even after the strike, he successfully cuffed her wrist with an old shackle.

"What are you doing?!" she shouted.

Locking the other half of the cuffs to a light hinge, Darion gritted his teeth, "As soon as I get rid of your sorry excuse of a man, we'll discuss where we can find the best price for you!"

Constance struggled and screamed, but no one could hear her against the storm's turmoil.

As Darion appeared on the main deck, he signaled the men with a nod of his head.

"Ah! Darion! We need your help securing that long cannon!" John shouted, pointing to some crew members struggling against the ocean's sprays.

The rain pelted John's face, and he could barely see his friend slowly walk past the cannons and up the stairs to the quarterdeck.

"What's wrong?" John yelled, completely oblivious to what was about to happen.

Darion approached John with one hand on the helm, the other with a blade to John's throat. Other crew members gathered around the two in an instant. Silenced with confusion, John could only stare at his betrayer.

"I want to thank you for helping us solve the treasure problem; we couldn't have done it without you," Darion shouted.

"Treasure problem . . ." John glared.

"We didn't know how to conquer the Isle de Flamo, now your usefulness has reached its end," Darion smiled as the crew chuckled.

The crew grabbed John and took him down the stairs. A few crew members along with MeLoy, ScottyD and Childer tried to fight but were vastly outnumbered and were pushed overboard into the storm's crashing waves.

"Constance!!" John screamed with all of his might.

Still shackled to the light hinge, Constance faintly heard her love's voice of distress. Looking around the cabin franticly, she didn't see any keys and the storm continued to rock the ship brutally. In a state of panic heightened by adrenaline, Constance pulled her hand as hard as she could. She gritted her teeth and let out shrieks of pain as blood streamed down her arm. Finally, her hand slipped out of the cuff. She made her way through the bottom of the ship as it swayed. She ran to the top of the stairs to see a crew she once trusted capture John. Her heart pounded as she watched their weapons aim directly at him.

"Don't worry 'bout your girl, John," Darion sneered. "Worry 'bout yourself."

With that, the crew members threw John overboard,

and Constance shrieked in terror. The evil crew laughed and continued to perform their duties, and Constance squeezed her hands over her mouth so as not to make any more sound. Still in disbelief, she watched as Darion took the helm with a smile.

She knew she wouldn't have much time, but she had to try to save John. Taking her cutlass from her boot, Constance ran to a lifeboat and sliced the rope with a single swipe. The boat fell overboard, and Constance strained her eyes to see the seven men out in the open water.

"What's this?!" shouted a large, hideous pirate.

He grabbed Constance by the back of her hair, but at that instant the ship was thrown by an enormous wave. The crew yelled in panic as the ship was tossed and the supplies rolled across the deck. A cannon came loose, rolled across the main deck picking up speed, and knocked the pirate down and Constance overboard. When Constance surfaced, she gasped for air and clung onto a piece of debris from the ship.

The storm was finally dying down, and the Hestia continued on—leaving Constance adrift. The lifeboat, John and a few of the noble crew members were nowhere in sight.

6

A year passed since Darion threw John overboard to die in the storm. It was at this time when two best friends set off to have an adventure of a lifetime. At the ages of eight and nine, Trace and Daven looked to the high seas for glory and riches. Instead they found nothing but mutinous piracy. They found no glory among thieves, and their young, innocent hearts bled with confusion, frustration, and fear.

And yet, during their time at sea, they heard of an incredible pirate. A captain so brave and true, who always put his life before any member of his crew, and never gave up. He was a hero. A hero scorned, nonetheless, by the other treacherous pirates at sea in those times.

"What do you think he looks like?" Trace whispered to his friend next to him scrubbing the deck on his hands and knees.

"I imagine a tall, dark man . . . with a big hat," Daven said with a grin. "Most captains have beards you know. It shows dignity and respect."

"What does facial hair have to do with respect?" Trace asked, immediately losing his breath as two huge boots bounded to a halt directly in front of him.

Two ferocious hands grabbed Trace by the collars of his shirt, lifting him off the deck. "You scrub like lit-tol barmaid!!" bellowed the beast of a man, known on the vessel as Crosset.

In a panic, Daven took his bucket full of murky, deck water and drenched Crosset's waist. With a terrifying growl, the tyrant threw Trace onto Daven and the boys laid defenseless on the deck.

"I fling both of yous overboard one of these days!" Crosset bellowed.

Trace looked up at the fiend, tears of anger in his eyes, "One day! One day Captain Rifton will handle the likes of you!"

Nothing but the sound of the crashing waves and wind in the sails were heard over the ship. Then, the slow pounding of footsteps came from behind the helm. Trace and Daven gulped as the captain approached.

There he stood, the notorious Captain Pernell D. Hoggard. The man was a sight of a black-hearted pirate in black boots with golden buckles, wind torn garments of the far east, a long burgundy scarf, and his shoulder belt holstered a silver pistol that had claimed the lives of countless men. His piercing eyes never strayed from the boys on the deck.

"Crosset, let them be," Hoggard ordered in his dignified fashion. "Boys."

The friends got up and made their way to the quarterdeck. With every step, their hearts beat faster and faster. Across the main deck and up the stairs the captain looked on at his men.

"Back to work you loafers!" he roared.

A quick turn and the towering man was eye-to-eye with the boys. "You best mind your manners or someday I will allow Crosset to practice his tosses . . . You both signed on for this. After only a couple of months you change your minds?"

Trace and Daven stood wide-eyed and silent, not daring to take a glance into the captain's fierce gaze.

Captain Hoggard gripped the two boys' shirts with both hands, looking them dead in the eyes, "I'm not through with you two yet! You best start to enjoy your days aboard the Hestia!"

Months passed, and Trace and Daven were not shown any more compassion. In fact, torturing the two became a favorite hobby for several of the pirates. The boys worked hard, in hopes they would someday earn their stripes, but in turn they were starved. Daven considered their treatment was the norm for a couple of cabinboys, but Trace couldn't believe for a moment it was right.

Most evenings the boys kept as far away from the crew as possible, hoping to remain out of sight and out of mind. However, in the foul galley of the Hestia, there was talk of more than just the two young recruits.

"Where do ye think they heard of 'em," asked Triggs, who had his smoldered eye patched tightly since his encounter with John Rifton.

"Any of de places we've stopped could have been whar . . ." the other mumbled. "He prob'ly is dead . . . you know how stories grow."

"We watched 'em drift off . . . no one coulda escaped that wicked fate in dat storm," Triggs said, assuring himself more than his crewmate. "He's dead. People just like to tell tall tales."

"Yes, but dead men tell no—"

Their conversation came to a sudden halt as their captain entered the galley. Hoggard's expression was a grim one as he slowly walked up to the cook.

"Don't feed the maggots tonight," he ordered quietly.

7

In the deep, southern waters of the world—where pirates sailed relentlessly—a popular port was the Ale'n Truth. Lewd women wore flashy dresses and poured ale down pirates all day and night. It was many, if not all, of the pirates' favorite place to go and forget the rest of the world. Of course, it was also the pulsing heart of any man who called himself pirate, and therefore a great recruiting location.

Strutting into the local tavern, ScottyD and Childer made their grand entrance. The two unshaven characters took a moment and looked around the place, as no one even so much as looked up from their drink.

"What do ye make of dis here scene, Scotty?" Childer inquired with wide eyes traveling the premises.

"I says we sit back and enjoy the delectable crowd before someone comes and spoils it'ol," ScottyD answered smartly.

"Eh?" Childer grunted with one eye on his friend.

"I just want a drink," ScottyD said quickly.

"That's what I thought ye said," Childer said already

striding for the bar.

The lads had downed several ales when a tall, dashing fellow of a pirate approached them.

"Well I'll be all topsy turvy if it tain't 'ole Childer and Scott-e-D!" he hollered.

"Mitchell!" ScottyD greeted with a big smile. "I ain't seen your unsightly mug in years!"

"Boys, I ain't gonna play games now . . . I heard thar was a mutiny a foot de 'ole Hestia and yous boys stood by a good man!" asked the large, friendly pirate. He recited his question just as he had heard the story, spilling only a few sloshes of ale between words.

"It be true," said Childer proudly. "Tat blasted, no good, smelln' hunk of sea garbage—"

"Hoggard," simplified ScottyD, "he organized de crew to side wid him during a terrible storm about two years ago."

"How on earth did ye survive?!" exclaimed a swaying Mitchell.

Childer put his ale down to talk with both hands, "You see! We was gonners. Tossed overboard by those cutthroats, wid de storm blown' down on us like the evil spirits themselves! We couldn't see a ting! Until, over the next wave, a lifeboat outta nowhere comes and saves us all! All of us, weren't thar 'bout seven of us?—Yeah, seven . . ."

ScottyD nodded in agreement, holding up six dirty fingers between his stein. Childer took a deep breath.

"But by golly, we was saved . . . We all think maybe thar was angels protectin' us dat dark night."

"'Ole Rifton must be steamin'!" Mitchell blasted.

The two friends looked at each other, then took a drink almost simultaneously. Mitchell waited impatiently for what the two left out of the story.

"De cap'n . . . his eyes lost their life that night," ScottyD said in a haunting tone. "Thar's nothing like betrayal I guess. He don't speak hardly a word to anybody . . . All this time, and only now is he ready to crawl outta dat bottle. He's recruiting as we speak. All de men he can muster to sails the seas again! But I'm a certain, he's got a lil' revengen' to do says I."

After only a short pause, Mitchell blurted, "Well! I'm sold!!"

He downed the rest of his ale, pounded the mug down on the bar, snapped his heels together and saluted the two degenerates. "Where do me sign?"

After Childer and ScottyD pointed in the general direction of their captain, Mitchell fell backwards to the floor still in full salute.

"He'll do," Childer muttered as he turned back to the bar.

8

Sailing proudly on the seas during this time was a grand brigantine known as the Great Blue. The old vessel was an experienced pirate ship, and was well cared for by her captain and crew. Captain J. Thompson was a mid-aged man with a proud stance. His gut may have expanded his wardrobe a few sizes over the years, but nothing could stop his love for the sea and living a pirate's life. One misty day, a couple of squinting eyes aboard the Great Blue spotted something adrift in the open water.

Bursting into the captain's cabin, a scrawny pirate named Phip panted, "Cap'n . . ."

Thompson stood from behind his desk, "What is it?"

Finding his breath, Phip exclaimed, "We found a woman! She was just . . . adrift!"

The captain didn't waste a moment as he stormed past Phip to the main deck. His crew was gathered around the still body of a beautiful woman.

"Stand back!" boomed Thompson's voice.

He knelt down close to her face, listening, then

jumped to his feet. "She's alive! Careful you sea rats, take her down to the doc."

The crew mumbled amongst themselves. Most feared this was a sign from the spirits of the ocean, and its meaning was discussed at great length.

Slowly, the woman opened her eyes to see a thin man in glasses and a larger man dressed smartly for the sea. When they saw she was conscious, they quickly went to her side.

"Don't be scared lassie," whispered the thin man, handing her a cup of water. "I'm Dr. Kagin."

"You're aboard the Great Blue ma'am," said the other tilting his hat. "I'm Captain Thompson, and you are?"

After shakily putting down the cup, the woman whispered, "Brisco . . . Constance Brisco."

Thompson put his hand on her arm gently, "Well, don't you worry. We'll be finding a nice, safe place for a lady on dry, clean land."

"Captain," Constance spoke strongly, "I want to stay aboard if it's alright with you."

Thompson didn't have to ask, his puzzled look said it all.

"I'm not new to the sea life," she explained. "And if it's all the same, I would just like to join your crew."

Kagin had a half smile, thinking of his fellow superstitious crew members. As a man of science, he truly wanted to witness the psychological mayhem of having a woman aboard.

"She can have my quarters, sir," Kagin said after a moment of silence. "There's an extra bunk in the crew's cabin that will be just fine for me."

"No special treatment captain, I can do many duties on a ship, I can work in the galley . . ." Constance was cut off by Thompson's nod.

"It's not me you have to convince."

9

Constance worked diligently and gained strength everyday on the Great Blue. Her soft, pampered hands bled most days and soon became callused. The first week with her new crew was an awakening to how spoiled she had been treated on the Hestia. Most nights she cried herself to sleep and dreamt of her John Rifton.

The young woman had lost track of time while she was adrift in the open ocean. After the storm, she learned how to handle pain. The ocean's salt water soaked her open wounds for hours without mercy. Now, finally safe, she believed there were in fact spirits in the water and that they had taken pity on her.

On the dawning of a new day, Constance awoke to the sound of wicked laughter on the deck. Putting on her belt as she came up the stairs, she was surprised to see the crew laughing, looking up into the sails. Following their gazes, Constance looked up to see a lone, skinny pirate who clung to the mast.

"What is he doing?" she asked the nearest pirate.

"Ole' Phip can't stand heights!" laughed the man, not

looking down. "And somehow his blade got stuck up thar!"

There was no question one of the wayward pirates had placed the knife as high as they could to watch Phip suffer with his fear of heights. Constance watched the poor man cling to the mast for dear life and wondered how he had made it that far. As the crew shouted facetious calls of encouragement, Constance felt an incredible urge to help the man.

Perhaps it was to show the crew her worth, or solely to help a fellow crew member, but even though she shared Phip's fear, Constance started to climb up the ratlines. The crew hollered for joy as they saw Constance start her climb.

"Don't worry Phip!" yelled one infidel. "You got a woman comin' to save ya!"

Phip was only a few feet from regaining his blade, but could not move his clinching muscles an inch. The further Constance climbed, the slower she had become. Soon, all the shouts from below were lost in the wind to the two. Phip turned slightly as he saw movement in his peripheral vision.

"What the devil do you think you're doin' Brisco?!" he shouted.

"That's a nice blade," Constance panted, "if you don't want it, I do."

"Why you deceitful lil' wretch!" Phip uttered. "Can't you see I'm tryin' to get it?!"

Making sure not to look down, Constance slowly made her way across the post to Phip.

"You're not movin' Phip," Constance whispered. "I'm coming to take something of yours, aren't you going to stop me?"

Shaking fiercely and sweating, Phip quickly pulled his head back to the mast, not saying a word.

"I know what haunts you," Constance panted again, "the same that haunts me . . . And I'm here to conquer it with you, Phip."

Far below, Captain Thompson and Dr. Kagin joined the crowd to see what the fuss was about. Thompson took off his hat, and squinted his eyes to see a man he had known for several years and a woman he had known for only a few weeks.

"Sweet Mary . . . What's Phip doin' up there to begin with?" Thompson asked anyone.

"He's deathly scared of heights, and what's better, he's even more superstitious of having a woman aboard!" informed an intent viewer.

High above, Constance began to feel queasy in her stomach, but kept talking.

"The trick is to not look down, Phip," she called. "Right now, all I can see is that blade . . . My goal . . . Of course, not moving isn't helping!"

Phip grimaced, not truly wanting to say it, "The spirits will punish us all for havin' a woman aboard . . ."

Constance stared at him, eyes wide as sweat trickled down the side of her face, then she began to laugh.

"Bad luck!" she exclaimed. "You have this vice of a fear, and you're thinking of bad luck?! What is happening right now, is completely blinded by what might happen?!"

Phip had never thought of it that way, blinking the sweat from his eyes. He felt Constance stand up.

"Fine! Rot here for all I care! I'm not letting that perfectly good blade go to waste!" she demanded, grabbing hold of a supporting rope above her head.

"No!" screamed Phip, as he stood up as well, grabbing Constance by the throat.

The men below were no longer laughing at this scene.

"Dat blasted blade is all I got of me father's," screamed the man in Constance's face.

One hand still on the rope, the other on Phip's strangling hand, Constance glared back at him, "Then go get it."

Phip turned around, took some uneasy steps back to the mast, and stretched forward to reach his blade. Constance watched proudly, still breathing heavily and looking up rather than down. The rest of the crew watched in astonishment as Phip and Constance then proceeded up to the top deck.

"Well played Miss Brisco, well played," Thompson murmured under his breath.

Phip and Constance flopped over the side and into the top deck with a thud, both panting and laughing between short exhales.

"Still think women are bad luck?" asked Constance with a chip on her shoulder.

"Yes," gasped Phip. "But you on the other hand, are good luck."

After a small moment of silence to catch their breath, they both started laughing again softly as they stood to their feet.

"Wow," Phip whispered, gazing across the endless sea and breathtaking sunset. "I've been on the seas for years and never seen it until now, Brisco . . . Thank you."

10

Back at the Ale'n Truth, while most pirates chose to drink their troubles away, some preferred to take some risks at gambling. More often than not, the stakes would be unbearably high and all too often the gamble could include a pirate's life.

Late one night, a group of pirates assembled near the docks. Under the soft, orange glow of lamp light, five rough sea faring men were playing poker and the bidding was on the rise. Rifton was not among them, but watched intently off to the side with many others.

A wave of low mumbles rushed through the crowd as a beautiful redhead approached the group. She was known as the Lady Emerald Delane; a woman pirates dreamt of at sea, and she knew it. And even more, she loved it.

Rifton saw her as dangerous, and yet completely predictable. When he spotted her approaching the crowd, he knew she smelled new wealth.

"Lads, who's interested in a rather large wager?" John asked quietly.

This question even turned the heads at the poker table.

"I can tell you all which of us will walk away with the Lady Emerald tonight," he smiled.

Though the crowd laughed, John kept his subtle expression.

"Yar serious . . ." said an older pirate known as Trillon from the same table. "What do ye want to bet?"

"I'm in need of a ship," John stated, "and if I lose, I'll sail for free with any crew . . . Make up your minds quick, because she's coming."

After a short moment, Trillon agreed, "I'll take that bet!"

John smiled, "It will be me."

The crowd roared with laughter, and John continued to smile because he knew it sounded arrogant of him. But he couldn't have planned the situation better as Emerald swayed up to the table. Her lovely green eyes examined the table of loot, but John could see she also examined each man's cards as she sashayed by each one. He waited until she was directly in front of him; up until now, she had no idea he existed. He leaned slightly over and whispered in her ear softly for a few short moments.

All the men watched with great anticipation for her reaction, which turned from sly to exasperated in a second. She turned a little, noticing everyone was watching.

Leaving the scene gracefully, the lady called over her exposed shoulder in a smug tone, "Give the man his ship, Ace high!"

"Dammit!" blasted Trillon, throwing down his cards on the table.

His fellow players were astonished to see he was bluffing with only an ace and everyone burst into laughter and cheers for John, the new captain of Trillon's vessel. They all erupted again as John shrugged his shoulders, and turned with a jog to follow the Lady Emerald.

11

The sun slowly disappeared over the horizon as Trace and Daven were finally able to relax after a day of hard labor. It was a beautiful sight of colors across the sky, and the sun reflected sparkles down a line into the dark, blue sea.

"What it is about a sunset that makes you feel totally at rest?" Trace asked his friend gazing at the scene.

"I don't know, but I wish it would sunset all day," Daven replied quickly, rubbing his feet. "I'm so hungry . . . do you think they'll feed us tonight?"

Letting out a long sigh, Trace felt a wave of guilt and regret.

"I'm sorry I got you into this, Daven," Trace said, not able to look at him. "I didn't think it would be like this."

"Hey, I wanted to come," Daven said sternly. "It was just as much my idea as it was yours so don't you think for a moment that this is your fault. We just got on the wrong, blasted boat."

Trace's eyes lit up for a moment as an idea crossed his mind.

"The wrong boat! Daven you're a genius!" Trace leapt off the bow and knelt down beside Daven, whispering his excitement.

"Next time the Hestia goes into another battle, all we have to do is board the other ship!" Trace exclaimed as quietly as he could with shining eyes.

"And how in blue blazes do we do that?" Daven asked in a disbelieving monotone.

"This'll work!" encouraged Trace. "We'll just have to wait till—"

Trace's idea was interrupted as Crosset slowly stepped up on the bow. The boys stood immediately, backs to the edge of the ship. The huge man grimaced as he held out two bowls.

"Cap'n wants you two stronger," he grunted. "You work like little girls . . . Any worse an' I get to throw you both to the sharks in shallow waters."

The enormous brute stepped closer, eye-to-eye with the two wide-eyed boys.

"And trust me, nothing would make me happier," he whispered.

He shoved the bowls into the boys' chests and bounded back down the stairs.

Daven gulped and somehow managed to squeak, "How do we get on another boat?"

Crosset's mood was obvious with each pound of his footsteps across the deck and down the stairs; he was on a mission to have a word with his captain. Fellow crew members, even some of the roughest characters, scrambled to get out of the gigantic pirate's way.

Bursting the door open, Crosset remained outside the cabin, "Captain."

His anger mounted to see Captain Hoggard casually

pouring himself a glass of bourbon. Even after so much time with the man at sea, Crosset was still ignorant of how well Darion could hide his emotions. He didn't notice the man's hand shake slightly as he poured, but he did see his evil glare at the rude intrusion.

"Soon, we will be passing through shark-infested waters," Crosset snarled. "You know how I love to feed the wildlife."

"On the contrary Mr. Crosset," Darion said in his most gentlemanly fashion, "like most of the men, you simply enjoy the sight of blood in the water."

With this said, his cold glass in hand, Darion plopped down in his chair and swung his feet up on the table. Crosset was silent, breathing heavily with frustration.

"Your hatred for the two youngsters is inspiring to say the least," Darion started, "and I assure you, someday, their existence will be insignificant. But for now, they will remain starved, but fed. The success of our voyage relies on their smallness . . . and yet we need them strong enough to be prepared for whatever that cursed island has in store for us."

Crosset's eyes swayed, feeling completely ignorant of the future plans. The attack on Crosset's thirst for blood couldn't have gone better for Darion as he took a long drink. Satisfied, he set down the glass and got up from his chair.

"You see, Crosset," Darion whispered, approaching the man, "that is why you are not captaining this pitiful excuse for a ship. Your lack of vision is always blocked by your lust to show everyone just how strong you are."

Only Captain Hoggard had the true ability to make a man about a foot taller than him feel completely small and irrelevant. Crosset finally found it within himself to look Darion in the eye.

"Now, was there something you wished to discuss further Mr. Crosset?" Darion asked as if nothing ever troubled him.

"N . . . n . . . no sir," Crosset stumbled.

"Good, now carry on and enjoy the smooth waters," Darion walked back behind his desk.

But before Crosset could leave, Darion called.

"Oh and Crosset," he glared, "never barge into my quarters ever again."

12

The crew aboard the Great Blue was a fine group of pirates who enjoyed sailing the seas with Captain Thompson. Though all were good sailors, one stood by his side the most—the new lady pirate Brisco. Years had passed since she had come aboard by accident, and she felt great pride in knowing she had sustained an even share of the work with the crew. Brisco and Thompson shared a love for glory and riches in a father-daughter connection.

On the dawning of a great day for sailing, Thompson and Brisco were arguing over which direction to take their next adventure.

"I searched those blasted isles for days! Thar's no such treasure thar!" Thompson raised his voice.

Pointing to the maps sprawled over the table, keeping them from flying away, Brisco kept a calm, yet determined expression. "The only people to have ever been there are those who laid it there years ago! They're all dead now and no one else believes it's there. Even you because you won't listen to reason!"

Taking a step closer, Thompson's eyes widened, "You're wanting to go searchn' de Isle de Flamo?! You're out o ya bloomin' mind woman!"

"When we get there, I know we'll find a way! That treasure is said to be the richest, fullest, and most desired in the world."

"Half de island is a bloody volcano Brisco, not to mention de evil spirits dat haunt dat place!" Thompson boomed. "When you can swim through that flamin' ocean, I'll be right by ye side!"

Beyond frustrated, Brisco beamed her bold, green eyes to the horizon without saying any more.

"Me lady, whatcha really aftar?" pestered Thompson.

Brisco stood straight and faced Thompson closely. "Captain, who on your crew is the most loyal?"

"You."

"Who knows how to read the waters?"

"You."

"Who knows how to read and write Latin?"

"You."

"And who do you trust most on your ship?"

This time, Thompson kept quiet, but half smiled.

"Thompson, my dear friend, I'm asking you to trust me. This voyage means more to me than what's buried on that island."

Little more needed to be said between the two. However, word spread like wildfire of the lady pirate choosing the ship's next destination, and it did not set well with the rest of the crew.

"Who's capin'in this here ship?" bellowed a pirate to Dr. Kagin.

The crew mumbled and contained a low roar

amongst themselves on the main deck. Soon, they were all gathered and there were clear, early signs of an uprising. Kagin slipped unnoticed downstairs and fled to the captain's cabin.

"You're needed on the main deck, captain," Kagin informed quickly as he swooped into the cabin.

Captain Thompson barely uttered his other precedence before Kagin took him by the arm and urgently explained the significance of the situation. As the doctor and Thompson reached the top of the stairs, their hearts skipped a beat as they saw the crew rallied around Constance and closing in.

"Have I not proved myself to you?!" shouted Constance in a terrified plea.

"You don't belong here!" a pirate shouted back from the crowd.

The disgruntled crew grew louder, and ignored their captain's orders to back away. They shoved aside fellow crew member, Phip, who tried to stand at Constance's side.

"Brisco!" Phip called as he was pushed to the back of the mob, "Up, Brisco! Go up!"

Constance was backed to the edge, and felt the ropes behind her. She took her friend's advice and started to climb. Just out of the reach of a pirate's swishing sword, Constance climbed as fast as she could. The sword sliced the taunt ropes behind her, and Thompson watched in fright as Constance swung erratically from the mast.

The men cheered with delight, but abruptly stopped when they watched the helpless figure slam into the mast. Constance managed to hang on for a few more moments before losing consciousness and she fell into the ocean. Before anyone could mutter a sound, a crew member dove off the side of the ship to her aid.

"Who was that?!" whispered several voices.

Thompson's emotions overflowed into rage as he threw his hat to the deck.

"You blasted fools!" he roared. "You've killed a crew member! A good sailor! A hard worker! A smart ally and pure-hearted soul!"

The majority of the men looked guiltily at their infuriated captain, as others continued to watch for signs of life in the slow-rolling tide.

"She was . . ." started a quiet voice from the crowd.

"She was full of ambition!" Thompson hollered, as his face glared red as a rose. "You all thought she chose the next stop for our voyage . . . Well, she only asked! In fact, she begged me to sail to the Isle de Flamo! Just like she begged me to stay aboard with you scum suckin', thick headed—"

Thompson was interrupted by a call from Phip to look to the sea. All the men fled to the side to see a figure fighting to stay above water. He was waving for the ship to come back, and Thompson bounded to the helm and spun it with all his might.

The men helped pull Constance to the deck, and gave the rescuer a hand. Thompson rushed back to the main deck to see a dripping wet Dr. Kagin knelt over Constance. Thompson gasped at the sight of her motionless body and a chill ran down his spine when he noticed blood on the deck. He looked up at the expressions of the crew and could not feel anger any more as he saw true concern on every dirty, sun burnt face.

Those few short moments seemed like an eternity before Kagin finally revived Constance, and held her head as she coughed water onto the deck. Gasping for air, the young woman felt a relieved and exhausted hand on her back. She looked back and slowly smiled at the doctor.

"I'm glad you're a good swimmer," she coughed.

"Unfortunately Miss Brisco, I am not a good diver," Kagin panted, as he examined his own leg.

The blood Thompson saw on the deck was from Kagin's unexpected dive off the side of the ship. It was a minor wound above the knee, and he was soon on his feet. Constance started to stand by herself, but was instantly helped to her feet by a couple of bystanders. The same crew members who had berated her moments ago were now standing around her in culpability.

"You really begged to stay abar'd with us?" a voice from the crowd asked her softly.

Constance smirked a glare at Thompson, who stood by with a shrug.

"I made a promise once to a great man," Constance started. "He's gone now . . . but I want you all to share this fortune with me. I figured I could keep my promise, and enjoy the benefits with a deserving crew and captain."

Shoulders sank lower in guilt as the men heard her words.

"Gentlemen," Constance encouraged, "I understand your actions today . . . Let me assure you! I don't want to be captain. I could not bear the responsibility or the dedication it takes. My loyalty is with Thompson, and I hope you all will share your trust in him as I do."

The men applauded and hollered in celebration, and gave three cheers for the captain, Kagin's rescue, and Constance's loyalty. In the midst of the merriment, Constance approached the doctor.

"I owe you one, Doc," she smiled in admiration.

"Look at this crew, Brisco," Kagin said tenderly. "I've never seen them this way. You're the difference, miss. You don't owe me a thing."

13

Rifton and his loyal crew members had recruited all the men they could from the Ale'n Truth, and had sailed the seas for years successfully aboard the newly-named Ace High. Small battles with other pirates and even a few merchant ships were their target prey. All the while, Captain Rifton remained a mystery to his crew.

Late one quiet night on the ocean, the captain laid on his bunk in his quarters as the sea rocked him to sleep. Normally, his crew's gabbling didn't interest him much, until he heard his name mentioned. Lying with eyes barely open, he listened to his crew's conversation in the forecastle, finding it quite entertaining.

"Whatever happin' to the cap'n? He be a gentl'man of fortune he is!"

"He's a fine pirate and a great man!"

"I never claimed otherwise ya scurvy wine weasel!"

"Thar ain't nothing wrong with enjoyin' a fine wine boys . . ."

"Me point being, de capin' just weren't born at sea."

"And you were?"

"Yar own mamma didn' wan cha'!"

"Shut yar trap!"

"Ah, da captain were a gentl'man. But he ran away from his landluber coffin for a real life at sea!"

"He wanted to earn his stripes among great heroes!"

"Den' why does he like you?"

"Eat char words and swallow yar tongue ya miserable wretch!"

"Well I hard de cap'n brought the whole mess o tings on heself."

"Any words against de cap'n is just a beggin' for slaughter boys . . . Captain Rifton is the greatest man to ever set foot on dis blasted sea and I'll kills any man dat says otherwise . . . He be a natur-al leadar says I."

Half chuckling, Rifton could recognize MeLoy's voice anywhere, and decided to make his way to the crew's quarters. They were still insulting each other, and throwing out suggestions of their captain's past life as he approached. Standing in the stairway, the captain's words killed all conversation, laughter, and drinking.

"It was a woman," he said softly.

All the men's eyes never strayed from Rifton as he entered their quarters. MeLoy stood up, but the captain motioned him to remain at ease.

"It's true, I wasn't born on the sea," Rifton said with a smile. "I wasn't chased out of my home, and I didn't run away from anything . . . I fell in love with a beautiful woman, and I followed her until the fates of this life tore us apart."

"Where did she bartend?" spouted ScottyD, who only wanted laughs in his drunken state. Though he successfully acquired his laughter in the bottom of the ship, it all quieted for Rifton to continue his story.

"She was a lady," he said proudly. "Make no mistake lads, she was a lady. Her life was all laid out before her, betrothed to a fine gentleman, and a home big enough to house half the countryside . . . But she just knew there was far more adventure out on the sea . . . Her wild heart was set on freedom."

It was here Rifton's eyes came to a tear, "As far as I know, she is dead."

All the pirates, who had robbed, cheated, and killed with nary a care, found swallowing a difficult task due to lumps in their throats.

"No! What makes ya think she's gone, cap'n?!" Mitchell could barely speak the words.

Rifton turned his back to leave, and left his crew with the words, "The sea didn't want us together lads . . . it wasn't meant to be."

The days went by, and after the story of the captain's awful experience with betrayal and love lost was known, the men expressed inspiration to stay together. It was a hot and muggy day at sea, there wasn't a cloud in sight, and the tide spraying softly against the ship and up on the deck were a pleasant sensation. It had been weeks since the men had seen another ship. John knew it was times like this when pirates grew restless.

"Men," announced Captain Rifton from the bow. "You have proven yourselves noble sailors time and time again over the years. That is why there is no question in my mind to share a fortune of a lifetime with you all."

This perked the crew's ears even more. A murmur rushed over the crew, but was silenced immediately as he continued, slowly making his way to the quarterdeck.

"I'm sure you've heard of it, some of you may have even been there; but I'm certain we can find the treasure of the Isle de Flamo."

The handful of men who had been with the captain since his inaugural voyage dropped their jaws in shock. Most of the others chuckled in disbelief.

"Cap'n! The treasure of the Isle de Flamo is a myth!" yelled Childer.

"It be suicide!" shouted another voice. "Der's evil dat lurks dat island."

Rifton smiled and encouraged, "Lads! Have you ever doubted me until now? I'm asking you to trust me. I would never ask any of you to do something I wouldn't."

After a moment of silence and looking at one another, Rifton put a hand on the helm.

"Those of you not interested, we'll drop you off at the nearest port. Just say the word and no one will think any less of you."

Rifton was extremely pleased to hear only the wind in the sails.

"Time to fulfill my promise," he whispered to himself.

The following morning, John was awakened by the sounds of screaming voices and pounding footsteps against the wooden decks. Rushing to the main deck, the captain was greeted by MeLoy, who was always ready to inform him. Ever since the beginning of John's life on the sea, MeLoy was the most honest and reliable man he had the pleasure of sailing with. They had been through all kinds of encounters together, but the ghastly fog that had blanketed the ocean that day was going to be quite memorable.

"Cause of alarm is 'dat!" MeLoy glared, pointing to the ship no further than a couple hundred yards away from the Ace High.

"She came about us in de night, hasn't fired a single shot nor has she run away," MeLoy panted, obviously distraught by the situation.

"So no actions have been taken . . ." John thought aloud. "I see we've prepared for battle anyway . . ."

MeLoy shrugged, "No harm in being ready."

John stepped swiftly to the quarterdeck, never taking his eyes off the ship. She looked fast and unquestionably powerful. John considered the vessel to be damaged, or perhaps uncaptained.

Soon, he noticed some movement on the drifting ship, and a stout man appeared in plain view, looking right back at John.

In just a few more moments, John watched the man he assumed to be the captain wave a bright, yellow sash in the air. John's men were now more puzzled, and stood waiting for their captain's orders—guns at the ready.

"MeLoy," John asked, "you've been at sea longer than I . . . what say you of this?"

The stocky comrade put his hand behind his sweaty neck, as if to pull the answer from behind his head.

"Seems thar was one time, when yellar meant a peaceful-like chat," MeLoy said, not fully confident in his reply.

With everything in perspective, John believed it. He quickly took the helm himself and steered the Ace High toward the peculiar ship. Now within shouting distance, the stout, young man waved the yellow sash once more.

"Ahoy there!" John called.

"Aye!" answered the man, in an accent unmistakably Irish. "Seems we've found ourselves in unfamiliar territory."

"Don't tell me you're lost!" John beamed, which

caused some laughter on the Ace High.

"Well! De smart mouth must be the captin' me hopes!"

"It is! I'm Captain John Rifton."

"I be the Captain O'Brilon . . . It seems me men have come down with an awful sickness and are unable to stand—let alone fight."

"Sorry to hear that!" John called back. "You look like a worthy opponent."

"That just be it! What say you I come aboard and takes you on me-self!? Just you and me . . . I never have crossed a ship I didn't fight in one way or another!"

"Admirable!" called John with a great smile. "I'll send a boat!"

MeLoy stood in whisper shot of his friend, "You sure this be a good idea, Cap'n? With some bloomin' plague aboard dat ship—"

"Nonsense, that man is healthy as a horse," John smiled. "And I like his spirit."

In no time, O'Brilon was aboard the Ace High with his finest sword at his side. He stood no taller than five feet, five inches, but his strong build gave him a prestigious look.

"Nice boat," greeted O'Brilon as John approached.

"Thank you, won it in a bet," John answered truthfully.

"Tis a shame I won't be able to hear dat story from your dead lips in a moment," O'Brilon spouted.

"Feisty lil' bogar," ScottyD mumbled to Childer.

"Now what exactly are the terms?" John asked, without a clever rebuttal.

"De man dat lives wins," O'Brilon chimed. "I win, I go back to my boat, your men lose a cap'n. You win, my men find another cap'n and hopfuly you'll leave 'em be."

"I must say this is an unusual circumstance," John smiled, removing his coat.

"Unusual times are usual times for me I'm afraid," O'Brilon stated matter-of-factly. "I've never seen such a sickness come over every man on a whole ship all at once. Enough of this now, guard yourself."

The fighting man didn't hesitate for a moment, as he drew his sword and attacked John. With barely enough time to draw his weapon, John blocked successfully but was charged again. The men all cheered and called out advice, some jumped up on the railing for a better view of the duel.

John struggled to keep up with his skilled opponent's attacks, and soon he felt he would inevitably be defeated.

"Move yar feet!" screamed Childer. "Dis' ain't no fancy fencen' class!"

Above all the clamor, for some reason, John heard this provoking advice and took it. With his feet now moving with each block and attack, John was able to maneuver around the energetic adversary. Still, the Irishman was an incredible swordsman.

The fight carried on for almost an hour, but the intensity of the battle continued to grow. Both of the men were drenched with sweat and their hands were barely able to hold their swords. They panted and continued to fight in spurts.

"I've nev'r given up befar," panted O'Brilon.

"I got . . . that," John panted back.

John helped hold himself up with the side of the ship, and watched O'Brilon's eyes flutter in a daze. All of a sudden, John knew this man wasn't just exhausted, but had whatever sickness had fallen upon his ship. The Ace

High's excited atmosphere turned to confusion as John quickly dashed over to catch O'Brilon before he passed out to the deck.

O'Brilon's sword fell from his hand as his body went limp in John's exhausted arms.

"Help me get him to his ship," John exhaled quickly to his crew.

Both captains had suffered some wounds from each other, but the crew saw the battle as a win for John. His respect for the worthy opponent was also obviously noticed by his crew. In the bottom of the lifeboat, O'Brilon slowly came back to consciousness. His eyes tried to focus, and he saw John sitting by his side.

"Someday, you will tell me about that bet," whispered O'Brilon.

John looked down at the man, "Absolutely . . . You're a great fighter O'Brilon."

The shaking man held up his hand, "Patrick, actually . . ."

Gladly shaking the man's hand, John smiled, "You'll understand if I don't stay aboard."

"Please," Patrick stammered, taking his hand back to clutch his stomach. "You just stay away and fear de day when we're back in full ability."

The proud Irishman waved goodbye in the distance for a short while as the two ships parted ways in the heavy fog. John watched it disappear from sight, taking the moment to appreciate the experience of meeting the great fighter. But he was sure he had not seen the last of Captain Patrick O'Brilon.

14

Back on the Great Blue, the crew was finishing the last tasks of another hardworking day of sailing. All were in cheerful spirits with such good fortune at sea, except one solitary figure in the corner of the ship. Constance sat on the deck with a sharpening stone in one hand and her cutlass in the other. The sounds of her violently running the blade over the stone could faintly be heard from across the deck. It seemed no matter how many times she slid her weapon over the stone, it refused to sharpen. It was the same blade that freed the lifeboat years ago, which she now believed was a useless attempt. So frustrated, with her hands red and her arms tired, Constance began to tear up.

Across the deck, Dr. Kagin turned his head toward the peculiar noise and saw the girl. He removed his glasses to clean them off with the bottom of his shirt, and squinted in her direction. When he saw her hold up her shaking hand to examine it, he walked over to her.

"Need any help?" he asked his friend.

"No . . ." Constance stated, then looked up to see

who it was. "No, but thank you Dr. Kagin."

He knelt down beside her, taking the stone from her.

"This isn't good anymore," he sighed, tossing it over his shoulder and into the ocean's spray against the ship.

Constance's shoulders sank, not saying a word she looked down at the blade. Kagin took her hand and adjusted his glasses to look closely.

"Miss Brisco, whatever has jaded you . . . it doesn't matter any more," he said gently, motioning to see her other hand. "What's in the past is past. There's no reason to dwell on it, and let it punish you today. That's why we're all here . . . living to forget."

The doctor stood up as Constance didn't move a single muscle.

"I'll be right back with something for your hands," he said, and left her side.

Constance exhaled slowly and felt the wind on her face. Hearing words of comfort was just as soothing as the feel of the ocean, and she knew how lucky she was to have such a crew, let alone a friend like the good doctor. Constance was certain the man wanted more than just friendship, but he was a true gentleman, and she never took that fact for granted. Within just a few moments, Kagin returned and sat down next her.

"This should be kept on overnight," he said, taking her hand like the countless number of patients he had treated over the years. "But I'm afraid I have nothing for this."

He had referred to the scars on her wrist, but she pulled her arm back with a scowl.

"That's from a long time ago," she said, "and I really don't want to talk about it."

"Pardon me," Kagin apologized, "but it seems for as

long as you've been on this ship, you've never spoken to anyone about your past . . . Not even to Captain Thompson. And I see it festering inside you."

"Only when there's nothing to do," Constance snapped. "It's times like these when all the work's done, night is falling, and everyone's alone with their thoughts."

"Aye," agreed Kagin, "and if you'll notice . . . you're in the same boat as everyone else."

Constance looked up to see several of the crew members gathered under the light of lanterns, playing cards and betting. Others were drinking and laughing, making obscene jokes together.

"Every pirate has something they regret and want to forget Miss Brisco," Kagin whispered. "It's all a matter of how they live, and how they want to die . . . And someday, perhaps you will let yourself live."

By this time, the doctor had finished treating her hands and calmly left her alone. Everything he had said was true, and Constance felt like she could finally begin to let go of her memory of John Rifton. At that moment she felt it would take the rest of her life to accomplish it. But, these men, this ship, it all started to feel like home. She took a deep breath and got up from her secluded spot and stepped into the light.

"Brisco!" greeted Phip with a drink in his hand.

"Lads," she greeted, while holding up her cutlass, "I need to sharpen my blade."

The next morning was a bright one. Not a cloud in the sky, and the men with ale still in their veins wished for some relief from the brilliant rays of the morning. Constance found the day to be a beautiful sight.

"It be another couple months sailin' Brisco, but we're

a gainin' on it!" chirped the helmsman, Squire.

As the wind teased Brisco's hair, she shut her eyes and imagined the Isle de Flamo over the horizon. Wishful dreams also pictured her long lost love aboard a ship in the shining blue ocean. This too-good-to-be-true scene came to an instant end as a screaming voice from the top deck snapped her eyes open.

"Captain!! It's the Hestiaaa!!!"

Immediately the Great Blue became immersed in rapid movement as the crew scrambled to their battle stations.

"All hands on deck!" boomed Thompson. "Ready the long-range cannons!!"

Constance squinted to see the ship turn to face the battle. Inside, the young woman's emotions set off a raging fire of hate, but she kept herself calm so no one would suspect her history with the ship. She could see, however, the Hestia was a significant threat to the Great Blue.

"Brisco!" bellowed Thompson, "Retrieve me glass!"

She followed orders with haste. She knew her captain's fighting technique was to watch his opponent's first move, then react. His strategy wasn't an aggressive one, but it had saved countless lives in his many years of sea battle experience.

Down in the captain's quarters, Constance searched for the telescope. She had it spotted and in hand when there was an enormous splash in the water no more than a hundred yards away. Through a porthole behind Thompson's desk, she saw the near miss.

"He's upgraded his long cannons . . ." she said to herself; for a second she enjoyed the memory of John telling Darion of the weak, old long-range cannons.

The crew worked vigorously loading the cannons as the young woman fled up the stairs. Practically tossing the scope to the captain, then running back down the stairs, the girl helped heave the last long cannon into place.

"Hard to starboard!" ordered Thompson. "Steady lads!!"

Both ships had turned, almost in a standoff silence, but that silence was broken as the mighty blows of the Hestia's long cannons fired again, and Thompson screamed, "FIRE!"

The roaring sounds of the cannon shots and blows to the ship rang in Constance's ears until it all sounded like constant thunder of a never-ending storm. As soon as the cannons were fired, she immediately began reloading.

Thompson smirked an evil grin as he saw the Hestia turn straight toward his ship.

"Reload boys and let 'em have it again!!" Thompson roared.

Again, the cannons set off their power in thunderous explosions. The crew watched in great anticipation as they struck the Hestia. Cheers rang almost as loud as the cannons.

"Shut yar traps ya bunch of sea rats!!" ordered Thompson. It was in these moments the real pirate came out in the old man. "Straight at 'em Mr. Squire!"

"Straight at 'em sar!" echoed the pirate at the helm.

The Great Blue and the Hestia came head-to-head, almost ramming into each other. As they passed, violent spurts of shots rang through the ships. Shots from rifles, pistols, thrown cutlasses, plunging swords, and anything else the crews could get their hands on were projected at their enemy. Some managed to swing and jump on board the other's ship to fight hand-to-hand.

In the chaos, Constance used the mast as a defensive shield as she successfully aimed individual shots with her pistol; she had hoped this close battle wouldn't give away her identity. But her hopes were dashed when she locked eyes with none other than Darion Hoggard.

She knew he had seen her; he had even stopped fighting. But when the two saw each other, the ships had already passed. Constance felt her scarred wrist, remembering that nightmare of a storm.

At the edge of the Hestia, two small figures stood together. As they jumped to board the Great Blue, a huge pirate grabbed one and threw him back to the deck. The other clung onto the Great Blue's railing desperately, screaming a name back toward the Hestia. Constance had seen all this happen on the other side of the ship.

As Thompson screamed his next set of orders, the two ships circled around to face off again. Constance dodged through the crew to the small person dangling from the ship, but she was not the first to get to him.

"What's this?" beamed a pirate as he pulled a boy over to the deck.

Terrified, the boy held up a knife.

Constance broke through the crowd around him, "You all get back to your stations!" she screamed. "The Hestia's coming around again!"

Like snapping back to reality, the pirates obeyed. The young woman exposed her empty hands, "Put the knife down, son. We're not going to hurt you."

Not saying a word, the boy turned to watch the Hestia. Constance turned to follow his gaze and saw the same, small figure being carried over the shoulder of an enormous pirate. She tried to watch but lost sight of them in all the movement onboard. She turned back to the boy to see his eyes filled with tears and hear his whisper, "Daven . . ."

"I want you to go down stairs, to the left and go to the far end, and wait. Alright?" she said as calmly as she could to the boy with her hands on his sunken shoulders.

He followed her directions, wiping his face as he left in a hurry. Constance looked up to see the Hestia coming for another pass. It was the same scenario, each ship taking a beating from the other. The only problem was, no one could tell who was worse. She kept her eyes open for Hoggard, but didn't see him as she tried her best to aim each pistol shot precisely.

After relentless battle, the ships came about for one more pass. This time, a silence crept over the waters and the ships drifted for a moment. Constance ran up the quarterdeck to see a quiet Captain Thompson.

"What's going on?!" she exclaimed in confusion.

Thompson took a deep breath, as his eyes never flinched from the Hestia.

"It's a draw . . ." the captain whispered.

Even more confused, Constance gazed across the water to see Hoggard standing at the helm, facing Thompson. Both captains locked eyes, and knew they couldn't battle any more. In order to continue to the end would mean their ships' destruction. These chances were not going to be taken this time.

"We will fight again someday," Thompson said in a pensive tone.

All of a sudden Constance's stomach twisted in knots as the Hestia turned to its original heading.

"That day might come sooner than you think . . ." she whispered, then wishing she hadn't said anything.

"What do you mean?" asked the captain, slowly turning to face the girl.

"That ship is also on its way to the Isle de Flamo," Constance whispered.

15

"You've got some explainin' to do," mumbled Thompson as he bounded into his quarters in a huff.

The boy stood with his head down, "I know . . ."

Startled, Thompson dropped his jacket on the floor as Constance entered the cabin behind him. All mouths in the cabin were open, but the young lady watched her captain's reaction; hoping for the best.

After only a short silence, Thompson pointed at the boy, "You first."

"I'm Trace . . . My best friend Daven and I were aboard the Hestia. Our plan was to jump onto your ship during the battle, but I was the only one to make it."

"Sweet Mary, he's still out in the open water?" Thompson whispered, ready to dart from the cabin.

"It'd be so much better if he was, sir," Trace said sadly. "He was caught as we were about to jump."

Thompson sat down at his desk to pour a glass of fine whiskey as the boy told his story.

"See, we ran away from home to live on the sea . . ." Trace was interrupted by Constance's soft laugh.

Thompson and Trace looked at her puzzled, and she smiled, "I'm sorry. It's just, my story starts out very similar . . . Go on."

Half smiling now, Trace turned back to the captain, "Daven and me never imagined it would be like this. We joined the first pirate ship that came our way. We were just grateful they wanted us aboard."

Thompson held up his hand . . . "How long ago was this?"

"About six years, sir," answered the boy.

Constance's smile immediately left her wind burnt face. Her heart sank as she dreaded for the rest of the poor lad's story.

"You think I'm daft!? You're no bigger now to be out here!" bellowed Thompson. "What the devil would that bloodthirsty crew want with you children?!"

"That just be it, sir," Trace stated. "We were really small six years ago, but they said it would be just about perfect to fetch the treasure."

Constance closed her eyes in disgust. "That heartless scum . . ." she whispered.

Trace's innocent face turned back between his two listeners, "I guess it's down in a cave, or somewhere the big pirates can't get to."

Thompson stood up, "Why don't you share what you know now, Brisco."

Trace's confused expression now turned to the young woman. Constance started at the beginning, but she managed to keep John Rifton and the promise they made to find the treasure together out of the story.

"All this time, and you still didn't think you could trust me?" Thompson asked, obviously hurt.

"In case something were to happen, it would have

been better for you to not know everything . . ." Constance explained.

"Why does everybody call you Brisco?" Trace asked.

Thompson answered for her, "It was my idea. A name brings a lot to the way people look at you. In Constance's case, calling her by her last name took away from the fact that she's a woman. And she's lucky the men didn't out right mutiny against me for allowing her to stay on board."

"Kid," Constance said in a shaky voice, "I feel somewhat responsible for what has happened to you and your friend, and I'm very sorry. Darion was going to use you both, and does not care whether you live or die."

Trace's eyes slowly sank lower, "Don't feel sorry for me, miss. Feel sorry for Daven."

The boy slowly left the captain's cabin, leaving Constance and Thompson speechless. Breaking the silence, Thompson whispered, "Kid's got heart. More heart than what could be broken in six years with dat wicked crew."

16

The Great Blue quickly made repairs and made haste for the Isle de Flamo. Constance only hoped they weren't too late to save young Daven. Every day, Trace proved himself a hard worker and pure heart. The crew took kindly to him and appreciated his help, and yet the boy looked completely alone. Constance exhaled quickly and fought off tears, for his loneliness brought back painful memories of her lost love.

"Any time now," Thompson's voice startled the girl and she kept her eyes on the horizon. "The Isle de Flamo should be in these very waters."

"Our tides aren't the only waters we will feel," Constance stated, referring to the oncoming storm and fog. "I'll go up to the top deck to be another set of eyes . . . One side of the island will have tall reefs we can't sail through, so be careful."

She quickly walked away from her dear friend, as he spoke to her back. "Someday lassie, you'll be able to face your demons."

The ship had already plunged into the thick, cool fog

as Constance climbed to the top of the ship. Her heart beat faster as she climbed higher and higher, but not out of fear. She was excited to finally see what she had dreamt of for seven years. This place was bound to be beautiful, and she wanted the best view the ship could offer. She reached the top, and hopped onto the top deck.

"Ah, Brisco," greeted Phip, "would'ja look at that."

Constance stared into the deep, red color of the fog. The terrifying feel and sight made Constance shiver.

"De devil himself treads these waters," Phip said in a haunting voice.

It seemed even the ocean was scared to make its sounds of splashes against the ship. Softly, a small boom was heard by all.

"Thundar," Phip sighed.

As the red color slightly brightened in the fog, Constance gasped, "That's not thunder."

The low booms became stronger and more consistent. Suddenly, through the fog, Phip and Constance caught sight of a mountain. It looked like it was bleeding streams of deep, red blood; every few moments the island pulsed with a low, thunderous boom.

"It's the Isle de Flamo!" screamed Phip, sending the ship into alarm.

Through the chilly mist, Constance gazed in terror upon the mountain of destruction, a place she had expected to be quiet and mysterious.

"It's not right," she thought, "this isn't how it's supposed to be."

17

Not far from the Great Blue out in the open water, Captain Rifton and his crew kept a weather eye out for the same island. Within moments, the crew's breath was stolen by the sight of the volcanic scene.

"Better luck next year Cap'n!" chattered ScottyD. "Don't like the looks of dis wicked fog anyway!"

Disappointed, Rifton cursed his prediction of the volcano having a subdued condition. He squinted his dark eyes toward the island's shore. There, between the rolling patches of fog, he saw a silhouette of a ship at anchor. Soon, the rest of the crew spotted it as well.

"Orders, cap'n?" inquired Childer.

Before he could say anything, a piercing scream came down from the top deck.

"STAND FAST—"

With only seconds of warning, there was what sounded like roaring explosions and the ship rocked almost up on its side. The blow sent most of the men to the deck. When Rifton regained his balance he saw another ship grazing off the side of the Ace High. In the depth of the night fog, the two ships had collided.

"This blasted fog, sir! We couldn't see 'em comin'," the captain heard from a crew member as he dashed to the main deck.

"Damage report!" John boomed.

As order was quickly regained, communication commenced between the two ships. From a short distance, Rifton heard a strong, answering voice.

"Who goes thar?!" bellowed the voice. "This be the Great Blue, ready yourselves if ye be foe!"

From up high on the top deck, Phip watched Constance turn white when she heard the next echoing voice.

"This is Captain John Rifton!"

Confused yet excited voices murmured across the Great Blue. Young Trace scrambled to the side of the ship in hopes to see the legendary pirate he had heard about. The ships dropped anchor and the captains agreed to meet face-to-face.

Constance slowly made her way down to the main deck, half-expecting to see a ghost. She had barely made it to the deck when Thompson was assembling the ship to ready for some visitors. Still in disbelief, she watched a handful of figures maneuver a lifeboat toward the Great Blue. By her side, Trace's eyes were wide and his jaw nearly dragged the deck.

"Welcome aboard de Great Blue," greeted Thompson, tipping his hat. "I must say, we've heard an awful lot about you."

With a charming smirk, Rifton replied, "I bet only half of it is true."

The two captains walked directly past Constance and Trace, and proceeded up to the quarterdeck.

Listening every inch of the way, Constance and the boy followed.

"If we can't see ten feet in front of us out here, I don't know how I saw them," Rifton said in jest, pointing at the anchored vessel near the island.

"This island's treasure is a myth, and yet we're here, you're here, and thar here . . ." Thompson said in an inquisitive tone. "I'm not a fool Rifton. Who's out thar?"

John took a deep breath, his eyes fixed on the ship's figure, "I only need one guess."

"Some things you could never guess, John," Constance finally said from behind him.

Thompson watched his prestigious visitor's expression fade from hate to a blank stare as he slowly turned around.

Constance's eyes swelled with tears, "I thought you were dead . . ."

Wide-eyed in astonishment, John took a step backward, considering this sight to be a dream. Then he stepped toward her silently. The loyal handful of Rifton's crew who had come aboard with him stood shocked as they watched their fearless captain fall completely helpless.

"I see you found the boat . . ." Constance whispered.

ScottyD smiled, "It wasn't angels lookin' after us that night . . . it was just one."

John finally embraced Constance and they fell into a deep reuniting kiss.

Thompson's hands flew to the air, "I give up! I give up! My crew fishes out this mystery lady, and she tells me not'in of her past! Just when I think I know her a lit'l after seven blasted years at sea, she goes and knows the Captain John Rifton!"

After a small moment of regaining his blood pressure, Thompson pleaded, "Someone please tell me what's going on."

18

"Watch your footing you filthy seadogs!" scowled Hoggard to his men as they trudged the rugged ground of the Isle de Flamo.

Crosset pushed Daven ahead of him with a hard shove to his back. Hoggard led the way, already starting to sweat from the heat of the surrounding rivers of lava.

"Still with us, boy?" sneered Hoggard, glancing back at a bruised and exhausted Daven.

"You said when this is all over, you'd set me free," the boy called up to the dark captain. "You gave your word."

"And you still have it my boy!" Hoggard answered back. "I've waited seven years for this . . . and I'm not going to wait any more."

In the back of the line of misfits exploring the island, Triggs grumbled to whoever would listen.

"Dis island be cursed," he whispered, in both fear of the evil spirits and of his captain. "They says de capin' dat laid down de treasure was more wicked dan the devil himself. Wasn't he Captain Darkhaven?"

With sweat beading below his red handkerchief

wrapped around his head, a crew member scowled at Captain Hoggard.

"Dat's right . . . So we got his evil being over us, and no likelihood of gettin' paid for it! Everyone knows thar's no treasure here!"

"What did de Cap'n Darkhaven look like?"

"He had a long feather in his hat, and a deep scar dat ran all the way down his face . . . Why?"

"Just in case I sees him, I wanna know who I'm lookin' at."

19

"As you can see the island is impenetrable," Rifton sighed, gazing at the pulsing volcano. "It's still too active and way too dangerous to try to find that treasure."

Trace shook in fear and frustration, "So anyone who tries . . . would be killed?"

Rifton turned around, confused a cabin boy would care so much about treasure. "Don't worry, I mean, we can all try again in another couple years or so."

Constance put her arm around the boy, "John, they have Daven—this young man's friend."

Rifton's shoulders sank, and with a remorseful hand on Trace's shoulder, he whispered, "I'm so sorry, son."

"That's it?" Trace squeaked. "Just, sorry?! You're Captain John Rifton!"

"What do you want from me?!" Rifton shouted, gesturing toward the island, "That blood thirsty crew is already on the island! And trust me, son, it's suicide over there."

Completely let down, eyes full of rage and sadness, Trace stormed from the quarterdeck.

"Obviously, you were held at much too high a standard to that lad," noticed Thompson aloud.

Rifton angrily turned to view the island, as silence fell upon the small group.

"Has seven years turned you cold?" Constance strongly asked, breaking the silence.

Rifton turned toward her, but said nothing. Much like Trace's exit, Constance stormed down the stairs.

As the dreary day reached its end, the heavy fog remained as a blanket of protection over the Ace High, which quietly stayed anchor alongside the Great Blue. Still aboard the welcome ally, John could barely see the torches of a tired crew thrash about the island. His heart grew heavy, thinking of the poor lad at his enemy's mercy. Of course the boiling emotion of betrayal had stirred his soul for seven years, along with the heartache of losing his Constance. Here he was, at the Isle de Flamo, with a great crew of men and his love restored. It all became clear to him, and he knew he had to rescue young Daven somehow.

John stepped down the stairs in a quiet hurry, looking across the ship to see if anyone noticed his actions. He ducked into the shadows toward the lifeboats quickly and quietly, now confident no one had seen him.

To his surprise, he saw the silhouette of a person already releasing one of the lifeboats.

"Taking one out for a late night ride?" John asked in his mischievous tone.

The person turned around sharply, and he wasn't too surprised that it was Constance. She simply turned back to her function without so much as an acknowledgment.

"Where are you going?" John asked, wondering if she was planning a naive escape.

"I'm going to go get Daven," Constance said without any hesitation.

This news practically knocked John down. In disbelief, he took hold of her shoulders, turning the two eye-to-eye.

"You were going out there by yourself?" he said, in a scolding tone.

Glaring confidently back at his dark eyes, Constance freed herself from his grasp.

"I'm not the same person you knew seven years ago, John," she said, now looking at the lifeboat. "It took a lot of work to get where I am now, not only with the crew, but with me . . . I know what I'm doing, and . . . and someone has to."

Constance was a different person, and John now saw that. It impressed him—she had even more fire than when he met her. Now she had the muscle to back her strong stances. And seven years without him, in this life, he suddenly felt compelled to fall in love with her all over again. Still, he wasn't about to let her go.

"You stay here," he said quietly, "I'll go."

"No," Constance moaned, "I don't want you to do this out of guilt."

"It's not out of guilt," John insisted, trying to grab the ropes from her hands.

"Yes it is," Constance fought back, holding the ropes further behind her.

"No, it's not," John pushed her backwards, reaching for the ropes once again.

Before the girl could say any more, she fell backwards over the edge of the ship. She let out a small shriek before the splash echoed through the ship. Half laughing, John quickly dashed to the other side of the ship where other lifeboats were kept. "Forgive me, my dear," he thought to himself aloud as he heard fellow crew members sound a "man overboard" alarm.

By the time Constance was helped back up on the ship's deck, John was halfway to the island, rowing with a smile. With every deep pull he took with the oars, another thought came to his mind. He knew his cunning getaway from Constance would have to be nothing compared to what it would take to rescue young Daven.

Finally, he reached the coast and anchored his small, yet important vessel. He could hear the familiar voices echoing through the cold, night air. They weren't too far away, but by the sound of their clatter, he knew they were preparing camp. As quietly as he could, he treaded through the island's wooded area, covered with sharp rocks and small, flaming streams of lava. He couldn't imagine what this place might have been like years ago, leading him to truly believe there was no treasure.

Soon, he was able to peer through some shrubs at the scene. The blackhearts had Daven tied and heavily guarded, as they guzzled their rum around a large campfire. John spotted a couple of the men who had helped toss him overboard the night of the mutiny, but he figured the rest must still be onboard the Hestia. His shoulders sank with a frustrated exhale when he realized there was no way he could free Daven by himself that night. His muscles tensed suddenly when he heard the booming voice of Darion.

"Don't exult yourselves yet you scum!" he shouted, throwing a bottle of rum off into the woods. "Tomorrow, we'll celebrate with the treasure in hand!"

The small group cheered and spoke excitedly to themselves as their captain left the camp, obviously to relieve himself. John followed Darion away from the campsite. Darion had his belt unlatched when a sharp knife touched his neck and the bottom of a pistol barrel was shoved into his back.

"Alarm the men and that'll be the last mutter you'll ever make in this world," John whispered.

Looking upward, Darion squinted his eyes in thought.

"I know that voice . . ." he whispered, slightly turning.

"It's me old friend," John smiled, feeling Darion's heart pound. "Back from the dead."

"I wondered where we lost that boat . . ."

"Enough," sneered John, adding pressure to his blade. "I could end this all right now."

"Why don't you?"

"You're not getting off that easy," John said, glancing behind him to make sure they were still alone.

"A bit bitter are we, Johnny boy?" Darion found a way to gulp, "Pirates choose their captains and crewmates all the time. It was really not that big of a deal."

"To them, no. But to us, yes Darion. It was a very big deal. And now, if you harm that boy it will be hell to pay."

With those last words, Darion turned around to see John was gone. He shivered a bit for a moment, wondering if it all had been a ghostly hallucination. But feeling the twinge in his back and the small cut on his throat made it all dreadfully real. The captain returned to the camp without saying a word to anyone.

John returned to the Great Blue and called for some help to retrieve the lifeboat. He lifted himself onboard to the deck to see most of the crew, Thompson, Trace, and a scowling, still damp, Constance with her arms crossed.

"Have a nice swim?" John asked with a smirk.

This question prompted some chuckles in the crowd, but Trace wasted no time.

"I thought you'd bring back Daven," he said, again let down.

John looked at Trace with great consideration this time in their meeting.

"I tried, but he was heavily guarded and I couldn't bring him back tonight," he said. "He looked alright. And we'll get him back . . . I'm sure they'll make their move tomorrow for the treasure."

"You could have been killed out there tonight," Constance said with a glare.

"Heroes never die," Trace said, smiling with a new admiration for John Rifton, the man, not the legend.

Looking back, as if he could see the island and the whole situation, John's brow lifted.

"Captain Thompson . . . I have an idea."

20

The following day, the evil crew, led by Darion and Daven, were panting and sweating with every step. Suddenly, Darion caught a glimpse of an opening near the base of the volcano. He turned like a flash, grabbed Daven, and swung him in front of him.

"In thar!" he boomed. "And yell back what you see."

Daven gulped and tried to wet his dry lips but it didn't help. His brown, thin hair clung to his forehead with sweat as he felt his heart race. In spite of his fear, he was excited to see this legendary treasure, but even more so, for it all to be over.

The ground shook for a few moments, and a low thunder rumbled through the island. Daven leaned into the cave's opening and slowly entered. He put his hand on the wall to steady himself, but pulled it back in a hurry.

"The rock is scorching hot!" he yelled back.

"Keep going!" ordered Hoggard uncaringly.

Daven could hear himself breathe heavily. The cave was dark and only getting darker with every step.

Peering further, he lost his footing and the ground gave way beneath him. Scrambling and hanging on to the edge, Daven managed to pull himself to safety. Looking back down where the ground failed, was a long drop with a slow-moving river of red, yellow, and orange lava flowing at the bottom. He looked around the cave with wide eyes, but saw only rocks and lava. There was no way around, nor any reason to search the small, sultry cave.

Coming out of the cave, the boy was greeted with "What are you doing?"

"It's a dead end," explained Daven, wiping his brow.

Grasping Daven by the shirt, and holding him up off the ground, Hoggard bellowed, "It'll be a dead end for you if you don't get back in there!"

Darion threw the boy to the ground, and at that moment Triggs pointed to the ocean, "Cap'n, look!"

The Great Blue sailed steadily and sure toward the Hestia.

"Move ya blighters! Back to the ship!" ordered Hoggard with a thrust of his arm.

Strangely enough, Daven felt a cool breeze pass, and looked to the skies to see dark clouds moving in. When he looked back he saw Hoggard and the crew had already left without him. Feeling like he could finally breathe after six years, Daven took another look around and saw a trail leading closer to the shore. Not wasting any time, he chose to see where it led.

21

The day's sunlight had burnt away the fog, but the ocean's winds were about to bring a storm. The Great Blue was ready to fight, hoping to catch the Hestia unprepared, but Hoggard and his crew had made good time in returning to the ship. They had already weighed anchor and released the sails as the Great Blue approached.

"He wants a rematch!" shouted Captain Hoggard as his crew prepared the cannons.

Squinting his pale blue eyes, he smiled, looking for his worthy opponent. His competitive expression quickly turned to dismay when he caught a glimpse of the man captaining the ship.

"Sir! It's—" stammered Triggs, one of the original mutineers.

"I know!!" barked Captain Hoggard in a ferocious rage.

Darion and John locked eyes as the winds began to pick up, and the waves started crashing against the ships with more force. Not waiting a second longer, John screamed at the top of his lungs "FIRE!"

The Hestia returned fire with thunderous explosions with each cannon. The battle was on, just as a deadly streak of lightning struck across the enormous sky.

Such a bright and sudden bolt of lightning made Daven jump out of step on the trail he found. He could hear the sounds of battle, but could not see the thrilling sight from his position on the island. Still searching for a clear path to the ocean, he started to wonder why. He was alone, free, but alone, on a small volcanic island with a storm on the way. And his only way of escape was to go back on a pirate ship he didn't know, or worse, back with the malicious Captain Hoggard. When all this became reality in his mind, Daven stopped in despair. He let out a sigh of frustration and thrust his fists against a boulder off the trail. When the large rock moved slightly, the boy stood back.

Letting out a small scream, Daven stood exasperated to see a full skeleton of a pirate on the ground just beside the movable boulder. He took a step closer to the pile of bones, and looked closely at the long gash down the skeletal face. The scar went directly over the eye, but there was no patch. The legs were sprawled out with a long rifle laid across the lap; Daven was sure the pirate was still sitting upright when he died.

"What were you waiting for?" Daven wondered out loud.

He proceeded to push the boulder to the side, and with a great heave, the boy managed to move the rock just enough for him to slide through. He stepped into the cave, which was brighter than the other he had entered earlier that day. Daven found streams of lava flowing slowly from the center of the island, illuminating the entrance. Further into the cave, the boy peered over a ledge to see a clear view of crashing waves splashing into the cave. The ocean's song echoed through the cavern, causing a low whistling sound.

Looking around carefully, Daven found the safest route to the bottom of the cave. He knelt down next to the water's edge; he could tell it was rising slightly. His feeling of despair quickly returned, and he wondered for a moment if he should end his life. Would it be better to end it all quickly rather than end up like the pirate at the top of the cave entrance?

"Daaaaven!" called a voice from within the cave.

The boy held his breath, as if that would help him hear against the tides. After a short moment he heard his name called again, this time it was closer and he recognized the voice.

"Trace!" exclaimed Daven as the tide rushed over his feet.

From over the ledge, appeared Trace's delighted expression. "Wait there! I'm coming down to you!"

Daven let out a laugh of relief, and wiped his eyes fast so his friend would not see his tears.

"How did you find me?!" asked Daven in glee, as the two friends were reunited.

"I saw you! I just followed!" Trace said excitedly, dripping wet. "Of course I had to jump off the boat, but I think they'll wait for us!"

"There's another boat?" Daven quickly asked.

"Yeah, Captain Rifton took the Great Blue, and we—"

"Captain Rifton?! You met Captain Rifton?!" Daven's eyes now bigger than ever.

"He's not what I imagined . . ." Trace said in a deeper tone.

"What, no beard?" Daven joked.

Smiling now, Trace continued, "No, no beard . . . but . . . oh my gosh, we got to get back! I bet they've made it back by now!"

Trace turned quickly to leave, but Daven's eyes stayed fixed on the back wall of the cave.

"Whoa . . . Trace . . . Look, at that . . ."

22

The Great Blue and the Hestia battled back and forth, both struggling against the crashing waves. The crews sharply performed their duties as the rain pelted down sideways across the decks. Soon, the two ships headed toward each other, grazing sides as they passed.

"Taste the bitter sweetness of victory!" yelled Captain Rifton to his crew as the ocean's furious blows hit the ship side-by-side their enemies' cannons.

"Tonight we will reap what was so rightfully ours seven years ago!" John shouted as he grabbed hold of a rope. Gracefully swinging onto the Hestia, he held his sword to Darion's chest, "We meet again old friend . . . but this time, you won't have the chance to do any back-stabbing."

Thrashing out his sword in a defensive swing, Darion took a few steps back.

"Why couldn't you just die?" Darion asked behind gritting teeth.

"I hear heroes never die," Rifton smiled, knowing the fact that his survival still shocked his betrayer.

With a great grunt, Darion lunged at John and the sword fight was on. The rest of the crew continued to battle, and left the two alone to finish their long-overdue duel. The two had never fought before, but Darion knew his opponent's skills were acquired in the past seven years.

For the second time against each other, the two ships were closely matched in firepower. But suddenly, from the other side of the island emerged the Ace High. Sailing at full capacity, Thompson captained his best during storms.

With another ship heading straight for them, the crew of the Hestia started to panic. In the chaos aboard the ship, no one saw Rifton's men disable the ship's rutter. It splashed the water's surface for the last time, leaving the vessel powerless to escape. From the island's shoreline, Trace and Daven watched the exciting battle.

"Look's like they aren't going anywhere!" laughed Trace.

The two friends smiled, squinting their eyes through the rain.

"We can swim that," Daven encouraged, referring to the Hestia. "They stand no chance against two ships and crews."

"I don't wanna swim anymore," complained Trace, still damp from diving off the Ace High.

Just then, the Isle de Flamo revealed how the island earned its name; a surging explosion erupted from the earth, and the volcano blasted scorching fire into the sky.

"Would you rather burn?" Daven asked, already stepping out into the tide.

"I wanna swim some more," Trace quickly answered, following his friend.

The two boys dived into the ocean as both ships started circling the Hestia. Hoggard's crew began to cower and plead desperate calls to their captain, expecting Darion to somehow regain control.

"Cap'n! We got to make a run for it!" shouted Crosset.

"They've got us surrounded!" yelled another pirate above the sound of the roaring cannons.

Though the Hestia began breaking apart, piece by piece with each blow, Captain Hoggard kept battling his lone enemy. His fury made him blind to the rest of the world.

Gradually, the Hestia stopped firing and the crew gathered next to the mast in surrender. Loud cheers were heard from both the Great Blue and Ace High. The storm continued on as Constance stepped to the edge of the Ace High, watching John and Darion battle.

Trace and Daven grabbed hold of the creaking Hestia. Slowly and carefully, they climbed up the side and saw all the men watching the two captains. Every scoundrel of a pirate that had mistreated the boys since the first day they were onboard was defeated with their weapons hanging from their fingers. Trace looked up in admiration at John's fighting skills as he returned each strike to his enemy. Darion pushed John back enough to take a breath, and realized his defeat.

"You did all this," panted Darion, "just for treasure . . ."

Captain Rifton said nothing, only glaring back at a man he once called friend. With all his might he swung his sword against Hoggard's, tipping it out of his hand and overboard—all in one motion. Darion fell to the deck as John held the sharp point to Darion's throat.

John breathed heavily, knowing he couldn't kill this man lying defenseless on the quarterdeck.

"There is no treasure, Johnny boy," Hoggard sneered with a half smile. "We looked . . . I even had a small, sniveling brat to get into that tiny cave of scalding rock . . . and it wasn't there."

"I didn't come back for the treasure," John boomed proudly. "I came back to fulfill a promise I made a long time ago."

Looking across the water, he saw Constance. She stood strong and proud in the rain. Even drenched from the ocean's wrath, she was the most beautiful thing he had ever seen.

"This ain't over John," Darion whispered. "Not by a long shot . . . One day, we'll meet again, and it won't be you that suffers—it will be her."

Hearing only an empty warning of a defeated man, Captain Rifton turned to leave the Hestia forever. With his back turned, Darion pulled a switchblade from his boot and started to charge. Seeing this coming, Trace and Daven screamed for their hero to look out.

John turned just in time to catch Darion's arm, and they both fell down the stairs. When they hit the bottom, neither of the two figures moved.

The storm began to lift, and only a light rain fell on the three ships. All was silent as Constance's eyes frantically searched the ship's deck for her love. Slowly, both bodies moved, and it was Darion who stood to his feet.

John's men stood silent in disbelief, and Constance felt all the air escape her lungs. It was as if it were all happening in slow motion as Captain Hoggard trudged up the stairs to the helm, took it by one hand, and held his head high. He turned to his crew, and with a deep breath he muttered, "Weigh anchor. . ."

The crew stood wide-eyed as they watched their captain fall dead before he hit the deck.

All eyes were quickly directed toward Captain Rifton as he slowly stood to his feet.

As loud as the cannons' roar, the crews aboard the Great Blue and Ace High let out great cheers and celebration. Hats flew and gunshots rang into the sky. Constance wiped the tears from her face and looked up to see the sun slowly emerge from the clouds.

Captain Rifton stepped over to the two boys who were beaming with pride.

"Gentlemen," he said in a serious voice, "I owe you both."

Trace and Daven, feeling honored by just speaking to this man, smiled big.

"We just wanted to warn you, sir, that's all," Daven said with shining eyes.

"I'm not talking about that," John smiled.

Confused, the boys didn't say anything.

"You both have shown a lot of pirates how strong friendship can be—and should be," Captain Rifton stated.

Now smiling again, the boys looked at each other and then back at their hero.

"You boys want to sail with us?" he offered.

Daven and Trace were astounded by the generous opportunity, but were still hesitant.

"Might be different from what you two are used to," the triumphant captain said with a sigh, "After an honest day's work, you'll get food, sleep and learn the trade of sailing . . . I can see why you wouldn't want to . . ."

The captain acted like he was turning to leave, but

the boys quickly pleaded they wanted to go. Already, a lifeboat was at the Hestia's side and Constance sat comfortably waiting for three passengers. The boys happily got in, and John waited for them to sit down.

"Rifton," asked a voice from behind him, "What do we do now?"

The captain turned around, acknowledging the other mutineers.

"Ah yes," he muttered, "the ole' crew of the grand Hestia . . . You all may go free."

"Could we come with you?" pleaded the huge Crosset.

"What for?" Captain Rifton yelled, in a shocked tone. "So you can betray again?! You all can choose another captain amongst you, rebuild your ship and sail again if your hearts so desire! Otherwise, sit here and rot."

23

In the galley of the Ace High, Constance was heading up the stairs to the main deck when she heard a faint hissing sound coming from the hull. She had heard the sound before aboard the Great Blue, and knew it had to be a battle wound, courtesy of the Hestia. She moved several barrels of gun powder to see the leak causing the noise.

"We don't keep no victory wine back thar missy!" called a familiar voice from behind her.

Constance turned slightly and smiled at her friend, MeLoy.

"I was about to go say good bye to Thompson and his crew, but I couldn't let this go unnoticed," she sighed.

MeLoy's brow lifted as he saw the leak, "Aye . . . well, you go ahead. I'll take care of dis."

Constance patted him on his shoulder with a smile, "Thanks, MeLoy."

The experienced pirate made sure Constance was out of earshot before muttering his bewilderment of how the girl found the leak.

Constance dashed to the railing of the Ace High, and saw the Great Blue turn to its new heading. She smiled as she watched Captain Thompson yell at his crew, and the beauty of the many sails as they caught the winds. She already missed the beautiful ship, and the lively pirates who sailed on her. Phip waved with one hand as he made his way up to the top deck. Dr. Kagin stood proudly with Captain Thompson on the quarterdeck, and they both made their farewell gestures. Thompson tipped his hat the very same way he did when she met him, and the good doctor made a short, gentlemanly bow. Constance never took her bold, green eyes off of the ship, walking with it until she was at the bow of the Ace High, and had to let it go. Soon, the ship was well on its way and Constance felt as though she might cry.

At that moment, John came by her side and put his comforting arm around her.

"Captain Thompson told me," John said slowly, reciting just as the old captain had said it, "that we would have good luck with this woman aboard."

Constance sentimentally laughed, and couldn't help the tear that made its way down her cheek.

"I didn't get to say goodbye," she said, trying to be strong.

"I'm sure we'll see 'em again," John told her confidently. "I've met some characters I wouldn't mind meeting again out here . . . this time with you."

Sailing away on the high seas aboard the ship, now in need of some repair, John held Constance in his arms.

"You still haven't told me how you got this ship," inquired Constance in a mischievous tone.

John grimaced about the day when she would find out the entire story of that incident, but they were interrupted by a couple of crew members before the conversation could lead any further.

"Pardon us captain," came the young voice.

The reunited lovers turned to see the bright, healthy faces of Daven and Trace.

"We were wondering . . ." Trace started, "Well . . . once a tide comes up, how long does it take to go back down?"

Extremely confused yet curious, John tilted his head. "What are you talking about?"

"The Isle de Flamo, sir," Daven smiled.

"Now boys," John stated firmly, "if you're talking about that make-believe treasure—"

Trace and Daven grinned at each other and slowly pulled from their pockets handfuls of colorful, stunning jewels, which sent John and Constance into joyous laughter.

"ScottyD!" yelled the captain to his friend at the helm. "We have a new heading."

THE END

Rebecca Haines is from Carthage, Missouri.

She graduated with the Carthage High School Class of 2003, and went on to achieve her bachelor's of science in mass communication from Missouri Southern State University in 2007. After writing for the university's magazine, *Crossroads*, and *The Chart* newspaper, she was declared outstanding graduate in the communication department. To date, she enjoys her journalism career with *The Carthage Press*.

After graduating from MSSU in the spring of 2007, Rebecca (Watts) married Chris Haines the following September. They now reside in Webb City, Missouri, with their one-year-old son, Nolan Paul.

Rebecca is proud of her strong roots in Carthage. She is the daughter of Steve and Vali Watts, granddaughter of Lottie and the late Col. Valgene Mathews, and the late Roscoe and Wanda Watts, all of Carthage.

www.ingramcontent.com/pod-product-compliance
Lightning Source LLC
Chambersburg PA
CBHW020628130626
46552CB00003B/1119